D0614352

WRITTEN BY
Lauren Johnson

COVER AND INTERIOR ILLUSTRATED BY
Eduardo Garcia

COVER COLORS BY
Overdrive Studio at Space Goat Productions

INTERIOR COLORS BY
Komikaki Studio featuring SAW33 at Space Goat Productions

LETTERING BY
Jaymes Reed

Sports Illustrated Kids Graphic Novels are published by Stone Arch Books,
A Capstone Imprint
1710 Roe Crest Drive
North Mankato, Minnesota 56003
www.capstonepub.com

Cataloging-in-Publication Data is available on the Library of Congress website.
ISBN: 978-1-4342-6490-9 (library binding)
ISBN: 978-1-4342-9184-4 (paperback)
ISBN: 978-1-4965-0094-6 (eBook)

Ashley C. Andersen Zantop PUBLISHER
Michael Dahl EDITORIAL DIRECTOR
Sean Tulien EDITOR
Heather Kindseth CREATIVE DIRECTOR
Brann Garvey ART DIRECTOR
Hilary Wacholz DESIGNER

Summary: Joe knows kung fu. In fact, he loves it more than anything. Every single evening, Joe walks to his neighborhood kung fu studio to practice for hours on end, until the day he arrives to find his studio is closed. So Joe decides to pursue his second-favorite activity: basketball. He joins his school's team only to find that the players are disorganized, timid, and lacking in discipline! So Joe uses his experience in martial arts to bring out the best--or beast!--in his teammates. Will their newfound skills lead to flawless victory, or will they continue to get beaten to the punch?

Printed in the United States of America in North Mankato, Minnesota.
122019 000113

PRESENTS

STONE ARCH BOOKS
A Capstone Imprint

BEASTS ROSTER

JOE

HEIGHT: 5 feet, 8 inches

BEAST: crane

FAVORITE BOOK: Jellaby

WEIGHT: 130 pounds

SKILLS: agility and gracefulness

TIM

HEIGHT: 5 feet, 2 inches

BEAST: monkey

FAVORITE BOOK: Troll Hunters

WEIGHT: 140 pounds

SKILLS: goofiness and acrobatics

OSCAR

HEIGHT: 5 feet, 3 inches

BEAST: tiger

FAVORITE BOOKS: Jake Maddox sports novels

WEIGHT: 134 pounds

SKILLS: ferocity and loyalty

KYLE

HEIGHT: 5 feet, 4 inches

BEAST: snake

FAVORITE BOOKS: The Frankenstein Journals

WEIGHT: 122 pounds

SKILLS: sneakiness and quickness

THOMAS

HEIGHT: 5 feet, 4 inches

BEAST: mantis

FAVORITE BOOKS: Enchanted Emporium series

WEIGHT: 115 pounds

SKILLS: quick reflexes and eye-hand coordination

In the final game of the season, the Cavaliers face the Beasts...
AS ONE, THE BEASTS ARE STORMING THE OPPOSITION!
THEY WILL GET THE GAME'S FINAL SHOT!

BEASTS 72
CAVALIERS 73
TIME 00:03
THE SHOT IS UP!

PLEASE GO IN!
PLEASE *DON'T* GO IN!

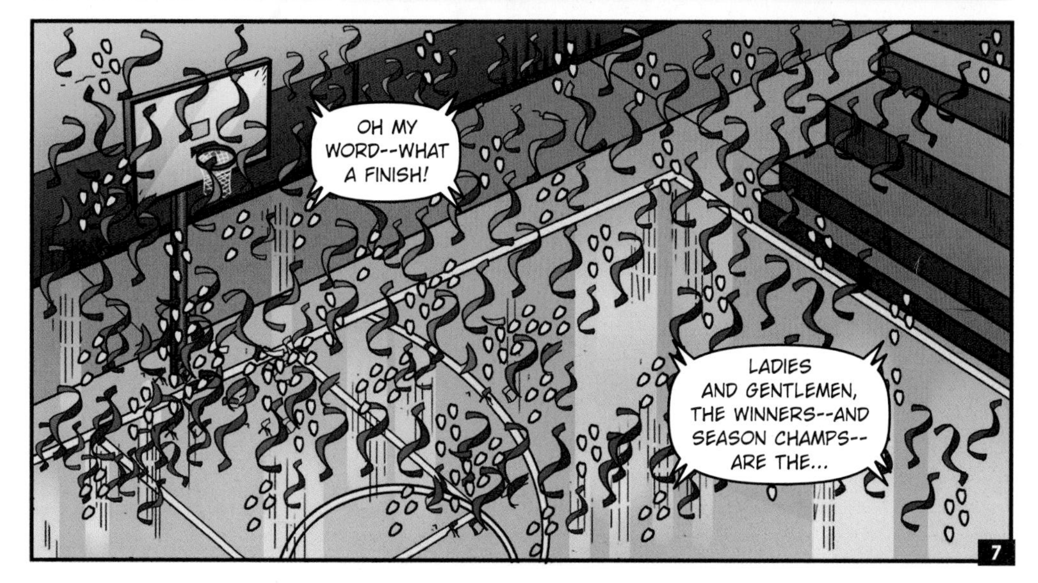
OH MY WORD--WHAT A FINISH!
LADIES AND GENTLEMEN, THE WINNERS--AND SEASON CHAMPS--ARE THE...

Three months earlier...
THINK I'LL MAKE THE TEAM THIS YEAR, THOMAS?
I DON'T THINK WE EVEN HAVE FIVE PLAYERS TRYING OUT THIS YEAR, KYLE.
WHAT'S THE POINT, ANYWAY? EVEN IF WE DO GET FIVE PLAYERS, WE'LL NEVER BEAT THE CAVALIERS.
NOT WITH YOU ON OUR TEAM, OSCAR.
SO WHERE'S COACH? SHOULDN'T HE BE, YOU KNOW, PRESENT AT TRYOUTS?

HE PROBABLY QUIT WHEN HE SAW THOMAS PLAYING.
HA! GOOD ONE, OSCAR.
WHO CARES WHY COACH ISN'T HERE? WE DON'T EVEN HAVE ENOUGH PLAYERS TO MAKE A TEAM.
I QUIT.
THIS YEAR, THOMAS QUIT BEFORE HE EVEN MADE THE TEAM.
HEH.
EXIT

OOF!
DUDE, WATCH WHERE YOU'RE GOING!
BUMP

HI. UM, MY NAME'S JOE. IS IT TOO LATE TO TRY OUT FOR THE TEAM?
WHY'D YOU BRING YOUR PAJAMAS?

PAJAMAS? OH, THAT! IT'S MY KUNG FU GI.
SERIOUSLY? YOU PRACTICE KUNG FU?
YEP! WELL, I USED TO.
LAME.

HOW'S IT GOING, FELLAS? EVERYTHING ALL RIGHT?
JUST SAYING HI TO THE NEW GUY, COACH.
HEY, COACH! THANKS AGAIN FOR THE INVITATION TO TRY OUT.
HEY, JOE! GLAD TO SEE YOU COULD MAKE IT.

FELLAS, LISTEN UP! THIS IS JOE. HE'S TRYING OUT FOR THE TEAM.
EXIT
HOW DO YOU KNOW COACH?
HE INVITED ME TO TRY OUT A WEEK AGO. WE MET OUTSIDE MY KUNG FU STUDIO.

WHY IS A KUNG FU DUDE TRYING OUT FOR OUR TEAM?
CAN YOU EVEN PLAY BASKETBALL?
YOU SEE, BEFORE MY KUNG FU STUDIO CLOSED...
GREAT, A FLASHBACK...

See, my classmates and I always met behind the building before kung fu classes started. We played basketball to warm up.

Our shifu, or kung fu instructor, originally suggested we do it.
We all loved kung fu. And we all loved basketball.
德
As it turns out, the two have a lot in common with each other...
PERFECT UNISON.
德
真
夫
壞

Our class spent most of our free time together doing one activity or the other.
Unlike some others studios, we became a true team...
...until the studio closed.
CLOSED

And that's when Coach saw me and asked me to try out.

SO HERE I AM!
YEAH, GREAT STORY AND ALL...BUT ARE YOU ANY GOOD?
YES, PLEASE TEACH ME KARATE, MR. BRUCE LEE!

ACTUALLY, THOMAS--YOUR IDEA ISN'T A BAD ONE. IT COULDN'T HURT TO LEARN SOME KUNG FU AFTER PRACTICES.
WHAT.
WHAT DO YOU SAY, JOE? WANNA BE OUR TEAM'S FIFTH MEMBER ***AND*** OUR HONORARY KUNG FU COACH?
I GUESS THAT COULD BE COOL. COUNT ME IN!
WE'RE DOOMED.

OKAY, BOYS, PRACTICE HAS OFFICIALLY STARTED. LET'S START WITH SOME PASSING!
At first, things didn't go so well.
DOWN HERE, DUDE.
OW!!
BONK
SORRY!
BONK

Practice, week two.
RUN PLAY #7!

UM...WHAT DO WE DO FOR THAT PLAY AGAIN?

WELL, THE GOOD NEWS IS THAT YOU'RE ALL PRETTY TALENTED INDIVIDUALLY.
THE BAD NEWS: OUR TEAMWORK KIND OF STINKS.

Our first kung fu practice didn't go well, either...
NOW!
OOF!!
KICK!
PUNCH!

YOW!
OW. OW. OW.
But eventually the team started to get better.
NOT BAD!
NICE WORK, GUYS!
NOW THAT I'VE SEEN YOUR STRENGTHS AS MARTIAL ARTISTS...
...IT'S TIME TO ASSIGN EACH OF YOU A PARTICULAR STYLE OF KUNG FU THAT MATCHES YOUR TALENTS AND PERSONALITIES...

"Oscar is a real tiger--
ferocious yet stealthy!"
"Kyle is fluid and has great timing--like a snake!"
"Tim is goofy and agile--a real funky monkey!"

"Quick and sneaky, Thomas is a true praying mantis!"
"As for me, I'm a crane all the way--swift and graceful."
INTERESTING...
LET'S PUT THESE SKILLS TO USE ON THE COURT.

We started with rebounding fundamentals...
HANDS UP!

...then moved on to defensive positioning.

Then we started passing drills.

Our shooting form needed some work, too.
EXIT
And we didn't forget to have fun.
WHAT A BUNCH OF WILD ANIMALS.
HMM...
EXIT
SCRIBBLE SCRIBBLE

One month later...
GREAT SHOT, TIM! KEEP YOUR WRIST LOOSE AND YOU'LL GET MORE ROTATION ON THE BALL.

ALL RIGHT, BRING IT IN, FELLAS.

YOU'RE FIVE VERY DIFFERENT INDIVIDUALS COMING TOGETHER AS A TEAM...
I'M PROUD OF YOU GUYS.

...AND I THOUGHT OUR UNIFORMS SHOULD REFLECT THAT FACT.
COOL!
THIS IS AWESOME! I'LL MAKE THIS LOOK GOOD.
SWEET!
NOT BAD.
WOW!
LOOKING GOOD, BOYS!

Game one of our season tips off.
THE BALL GOES TO THE KNIGHTS.
BEASTS
KNIGHTS
0
0
HE SHOOTS...

BEASTS 0
KNIGHTS 2
...HE SCORES!
NICE SHOT!
BETTER PASS!
OSCAR OF THE BEASTS CHARGES...

OSCAR GOES FOR A LAYUP...
EXIT

...AND
SINKS THE
SHOT!
AND WE'RE
ON THE
SCOREBOARD!
2
2
THE TIGER
STRIKES!
THANKS,
DUDES!
HAHA!
ENTER: THE
TIGER!
NICE
WORK,
OSCAR.
I DON'T
HAVE ANY
KUNG FU
JOKES.

THE KNIGHTS ARE CRUISING DOWN THE COURT!
HE DRIVES IN FOR A LAYUP--

WOW! KYLE COMES OUT OF NOWHERE TO STEAL THE BALL MID-PLAY!
THAT KID IS AS QUICK AS A SNAKE.
INDEED!
Later that game...
KYLE PASSES...
CATCH!

THE BEASTS PUSH THE BALL UP THE COURT.
BEASTS
KNIGHTS
JOE DRIVES TO THE RIM...
HE SHOOTS...!

OH! HE MISSED!
CLANG!
WAS THAT A DUNK ATTEMPT? AT HIS AGE?!
SHAKE IT OFF, JOE! GET BACK ON 'D!'

WITH THAT BASKET, THE KNIGHTS HAVE PULLED AHEAD.
EXIT
GET BACK ON DEFENSE FASTER, BEASTS!
I'M OPEN!

TIM!!
BEAST
KNIGH

BEASTS
KNIGHTS
TIM IS PULLING OFF SOME STRANGE MOVES OUT THERE!

BUT HE SINKS A HOOK SHOT!
NICE MOVES, MONKEY MAN!
THANKS!
ONLY TWENTY SECONDS LEFT ON THE CLOCK!
THE KNIGHTS HAVE THE BALL. THE BEASTS ARE DOWN BY ONE!
JOE ELEGANTLY BLOCKS THE SHOT!

WITH LITTLE TIME REMAINING, THE BEASTS CHARGE DOWN THE COURT!
THIS WILL BE THE LAST PLAY OF THE GAME, FOLKS!
WOOSH
FWOOSH

WHAT AN AMAZING DISPLAY OF PASSING!
BEASTS 72
KNIGHTS 71
BZZZZZZZT!
THE BEASTS WIN THE FIRST GAME OF THE SEASON!

GREAT JOB, BOYS!
YOU PLAYED VERY MUCH LIKE A TEAM, ESPECIALLY ON THAT LAST PLAY.
I'M PROUD OF YOUR EFFORTS TONIGHT.
PLEASE GET DOWN FROM THERE, TIM.

PSST. JOE, ARE YOU CRAZY? WHAT WAS WITH THAT DUNK ATTEMPT?
I'VE BEEN PRACTICING MY CRANE SLAM FOR MONTHS.
I'VE NEVER PULLED IT OFF BEFORE, BUT I THOUGHT I COULD TONIGHT...
YOUR LITTLE STUNT ALMOST COST US THE GAME.
SORRY.

Later, on the drive back to school...

HEY JOE, GOT A SECOND?
OH, UM. SURE.
I'M LOOKING FOR FEEDBACK ON MY RECENT SKETCHES.

WOW! THEY'RE AMAZING!
!!

IS THIS HOW YOU CAME UP WITH THE IDEA FOR OUR UNIFORMS?
YEP. WHAT CAN I SAY, YOU INSPIRED ME--AND THE TEAM.
HERE, THIS IS FOR YOU.

THANKS, COACH!

COOL.

The next few games flew by...
BEASTS
COW
62
60
THE BEASTS WIN THEIR SECOND GAME IN A ROW!
THE BEASTS WIN THEIR THIRD STRAIGHT GAME. THEY'RE OFFICIALLY ON A STREAK!
THE BEASTS WIN THEIR FOURTH GAME IN A ROW!
BEASTS
GIANTS
79
70
EXIT
G

THE BEASTS SIMPLY CANNOT BE STOPPED!
BEASTS 83
BADGERS 80

BEASTS 90
WILDCATS 79
IT'S A BLOWOUT WIN FOR THE BEASTS!

YET ANOTHER BIG WIN FOR THE BEASTS!
THEY'LL BE UNDEFEATED GOING INTO THE FINAL GAME OF THE SEASON AGAINST THE ALSO UNDEFEATED CAVALIERS!

The day before the season's last game...
BEAS

BEASTS

Now.
HEY GUYS, SORRY I'M LATE!

EXIT
NO WORRIES, WE'RE JUST WARMING UP!
BRING IT IN, BOYS!

TIP-OFF IS IN A FEW MINUTES. I KNOW THIS IS THE FINAL GAME OF THE SEASON, SO I SHOULD PROBABLY GIVE A SPEECH.
I'LL JUST SAY THAT IT HAS BEEN AN HONOR TO COACH YOU GUYS.
TEAM ON THREE?
BEASTS

TEAM!
TEAM!

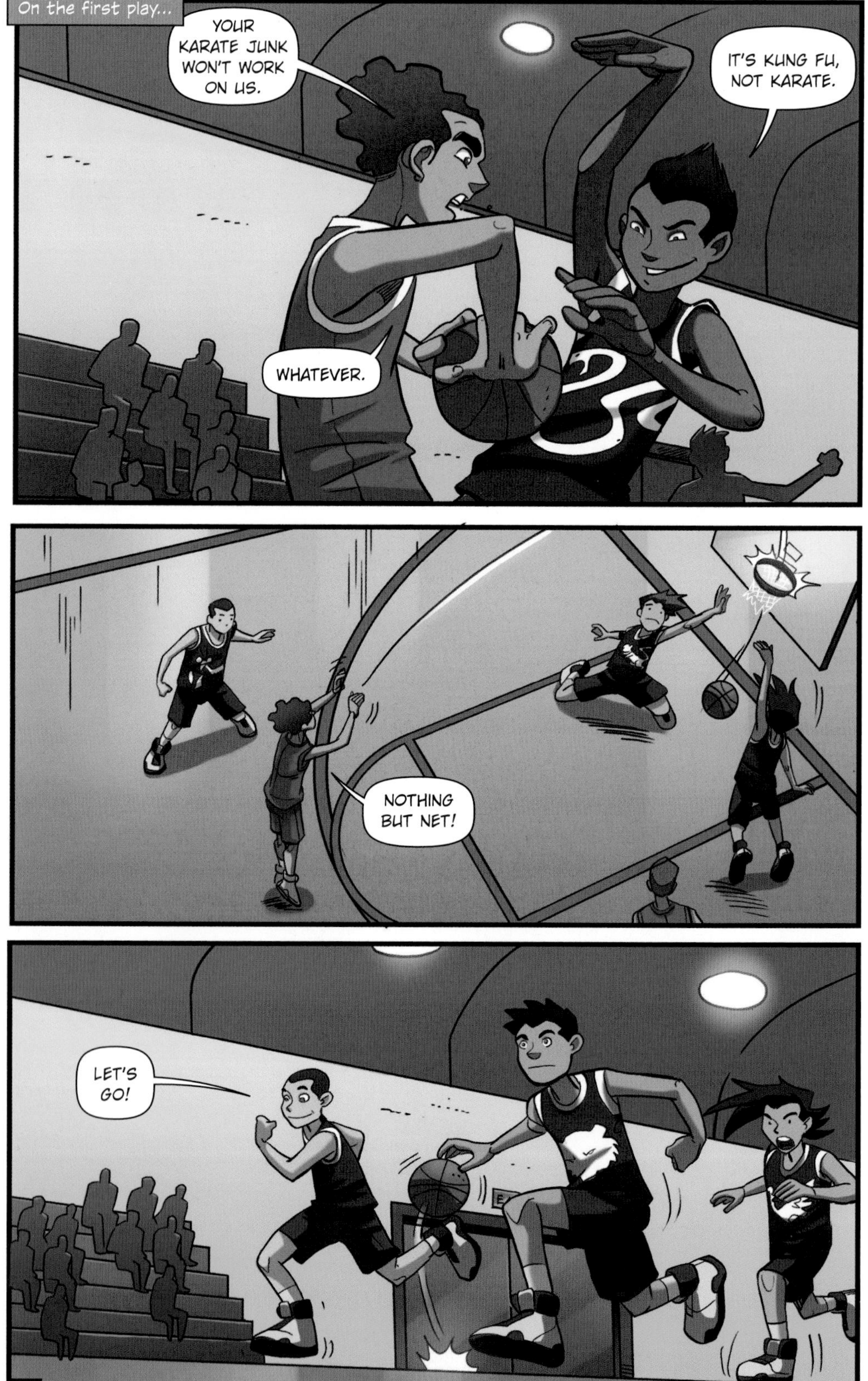
On the first play...
YOUR KARATE JUNK WON'T WORK ON US.
IT'S KUNG FU, NOT KARATE.
WHATEVER.
NOTHING BUT NET!
LET'S GO!

REJECTED!
I GOT IT!

I'M OPEN!

SWISH
THE BEASTS SCORE WITH AN IMPRESSIVE EFFORT FROM KYLE!
A moment later...
SWISH
AND THE CAVALIERS SINK A THREE-POINTER!
WHAT AN INTENSE GAME!
HALF-TIME IS UPON US. SO FAR, THE CAVALIERS AND THE BEASTS ARE TREATING US TO QUITE A SHOW.

Later...
YOU KNOW WHAT TO DO, JOE.
I DO.
GO WILD, BEASTS!

LET'S GET YOU AIRBORNE!
FWOOSH

WOW!!
IS THAT EVEN LEGAL?!
I'M NOT SURE.

...
BUT IT WAS PRETTY CREATIVE TEAMWORK.
I'LL ALLOW IT.

I FINALLY DID IT! I HIT MY CRANE SLAM! THANKS, DUDE!
NO PROBLEM. I JUST FIGURED YOU COULD USE A LEG UP.
Moments later...
A STEAL BY THE BEASTS!
PRESS
ANOTHER GREAT PASS BY TIM!

AND KYLE HITS A SNEAKY JUMPER!
THAT PUTS THE BEASTS WITHIN ONE POINT OF THE CAVALIERS!
YESSSSS!

TIME OUT!!
ONLY TEN SECONDS LEFT IN THE GAME, AND THE CAVS HAVE THE BALL. WE'LL NEED TO GET CREATIVE TO WIN. ANY IDEAS, JOE?
I SAY WE LET THE MANTIS MAKE THE CALL. WE'LL NEED SOMETHING CLEVER TO PULL THIS WIN OUT.
ME?
SOUNDS GOOD TO ME. IT'S ALL UP TO YOU, THOMAS.

OKAY, THEN. HERE'S WHAT WE'LL DO...
Thomas's plan was simple but brilliant.
WHISPER
WHISPER
First, we left their worst shooter wide open...
He couldn't NOT take the wide-open shot.

Sure enough, he missed--and we snagged the rebound!
TIME
00:07
72
BEASTS
73
CAVALIERS
From that point, it was a matter of quick passing...
TIME
00:05

BOUNCE!
WOOSH
...and teamwork.

FLICK
THE SHOT IS IN THE AIR AT THE BUZZER!
BZZZZZZZT!
GASP!
GO IN!!

GASP! WHAT A FINISH!!!
LADIES AND GENTLEMEN, THE WINNERS-- AND SEASON CHAMPIONS-- ARE...
74
BEASTS
73
CAVALIERS
...THE BEASTS!!!
EXIT
NICE MOVES, MANTIS!
WHAT CAN I SAY? I'M A BEAST!
JUST LIKE THE REST OF US!

ABOUT THE AUTHOR

LAUREN JOHNSON is a freelance writer and editor living and working in North Carolina. In her spare time she likes to read, paint, and practice marital arts moves--just like the moves found in this book.

ABOUT THE ILLUSTRATOR

Working out of Mexico City, **EDUARDO GARCIA** has lent his illustration talents to such varied projects as the Spider-Man Family, Flash Gordon, and Speed Racer. He's currently working on a series of illustrations for an educational publisher while his wife and children look over his shoulder!

ABOUT THE LETTERER

JAYMES REED has operated the company Digital-CAPS: Comic Book Lettering since 2003. He has done lettering for many publishers, most notably and recently Avatar Press. He's also the only letterer working with Inception Strategies, an Aboriginal-Australian publisher that develops social comics with public service messages for the Australian government. Jaymes also a 2012 & 2013 Shel Dorf Award Nominee.

GLOSSARY

AGILE (AJ-uhl)—able to move quickly and easily

BRILLIANT (BRILL-yuhnt)—very impressive or intelligent

ELEGANTLY (EL-uh-guhnt-lee)—graceful and poised

FEROCIOUS (fuh-ROH-shuhss)—very fierce, intense, or violent

FUNDAMENTALS (fun-duh-MEN-tuhls)—the basic and important parts of something

HONORARY (ON-uh-rare-ee)—given as a sign of honor or achievement, or regarded as one of a group although not officially elected or included

INTENSE (in-TENSS)—with great effort or seriousness

OPPOSITION (op-uh-ZISH-uhn)—a person or group that you are trying to defeat or succeed against

REFLECT (ri-FLEKT)—to show an idea through action

REJECTED (ri-JEK-tid)—denied. In basketball, getting "rejected" is slang for having a shot blocked

STEALTHY (STELL-thee)—quietly and sneakily

UNISON (YOO-niss-uhn)—together as one

VISUAL QUESTIONS

1. What do you think Coach is scribbling on his clipboard in this panel? Explain your answer.

2. What do the things that Joe keeps in his room say about him as a person?

3. What do the little birds floating around Joe's head mean? Reread pages 34-35 if you aren't certain.

4. If you could choose any animal to be like, what animal would you choose? Why?

5. What happened in this panel? How do you know what happened? Explain your answer.

6. This panel shows two Beasts working together to accomplish something. Identify three other panels in this book that show the characters demonstrating good teamwork.

READ THEM ALL!

8-BIT BASEBALL

Jared Richards is undefeated in baseball games--video games, anyway. But when he loses a bet to his best friend, Jared is forced to get off the couch and step onto the field for his school's baseball team tryouts. Despite the fact that he's never even held a baseball before, Jared ends up being pretty impressive as a pitcher--until the line between video games and reality begins to blur. Can Jared sort out the glitch in his brain before he blows the big game?

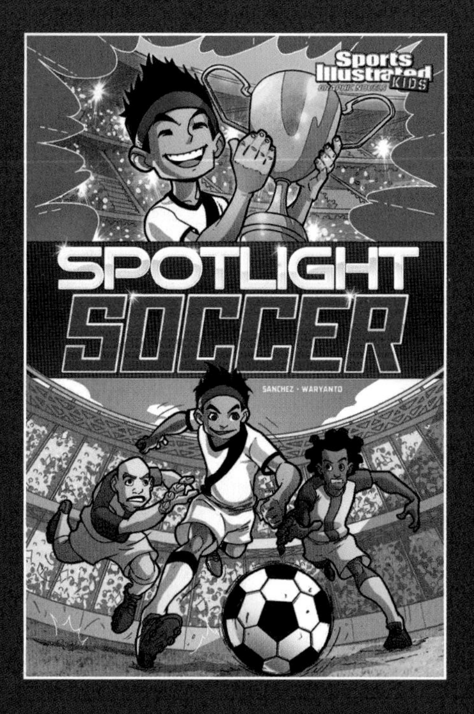

SPOTLIGHT SOCCER

More than anything else, Franco dreams of going pro some day. After all, his soccer coaches say he's the best kind of player: more giving than greedy, preferring to rack up the assists instead of scoring goals. And that method works just fine until Franco has to change schools. On his new team, Franco's pass-first approach to soccer just isn't working. To make matters worse, the team is filled with ball-hogs. Franco refuses to let his dream of going pro die, but the new team is pretty much a living nightmare.

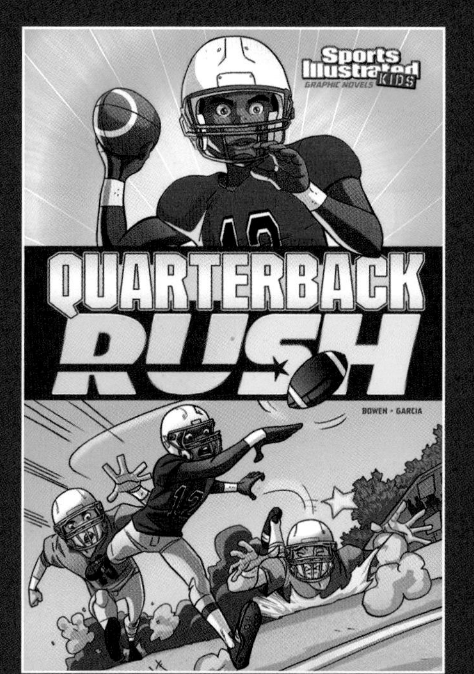

QUARTERBACK RUSH

The Otters are absolutely awesome in practice. Everyone's talented and determined, and their new quarterback, Aaron Corbin, throws bullets . . . so why are the Otters struggling to win games? Steve Michaels, one of the team's receivers, notices that Aaron seems to be afraid of getting hit. With a little help from his teammates, Steve goes to great lengths to toughen up Aaron only to discover that toughness isn't the quarterback's actual problem.